Molly Mischief

My Perfect Pet

GROSSET & DUNLAP
Penguin Young Readers Group
An Imprint of Penguin Random House LLC

Copyright © 2017 by Adam Hargreaves. All rights reserved. First published in the United Kingdom in 2017 by Pavilion Books Limited. First published in the United States in 2019 by Grosset & Dunlap, an imprint of Penguin Random House LLC, 345 Hudson Street, New York, New York 10014. GROSSET & DUNLAP is a trademark of Penguin Random House LLC. Manufactured in China.

Library of Congress Cataloging-in-Publication Data is available.

ISBN 9781524788025   10 9 8 7 6 5 4 3 2 1

Molly Mischief

My Perfect Pet

Adam Hargreaves

Grosset & Dunlap
An Imprint of Penguin Random House

Hello, my name is **Molly**.
Sometimes people call me **Molly Mischief.**

I have **lots** of ideas.
I think they are very good ideas, but not everyone agrees.
I know my mom and dad don't agree when they shout
my name **very** loudly . . . that happens a lot.

MOLLY!

Today my dad took me and
my brother to the zoo.

We saw lots of different animals.
My brother liked the warthogs best
of all. They are **nearly** as ugly as he is.

I got into trouble at the zoo.

Molly!

Don't tickle the penguin!

Molly!

Don't chase the parrot!

Molly!

Don't wake up the flamingo!

Molly!

Don't feed the crocodile!

And then I found a hippopotamus.
It was very big.

Much bigger than my pet mouse, Polka.
She is tiny.

I wish I had a big pet.
A big pet like a hippo.

I took the hippo home.

Molly!

But my mom and dad weren't very happy
about my new pet.
So I had to take the hippo back to the zoo.

If I can't have a hippo,
then I wonder what other pet I could have . . .

I like bears. How about a big bear?

There was a polar bear at the zoo.

I took the polar bear home.

But polar bears like the cold, and my bedroom was too hot.
And I don't think a polar bear would fit in the fridge.

I had to take the polar bear back to the zoo.

**At the zoo I also saw a giraffe—the tallest animal in the world.
I took the giraffe home.**

But the giraffe would not fit in my bedroom.
I had to cut a hole in the roof.
Dad was not very happy about that.

Molly!

I had to take the giraffe
back to the zoo.

My family is very hard to please.

I had to take the tiger back to the zoo, too.

And the rhino.

And the walrus.

And the ostrich.

And the anaconda.

I want a big pet.
A large pet.
A giant pet.
A huge pet.

And then I found just
what I was looking for.

An elephant!

Now, that would be
a big pet.

So I took it home.

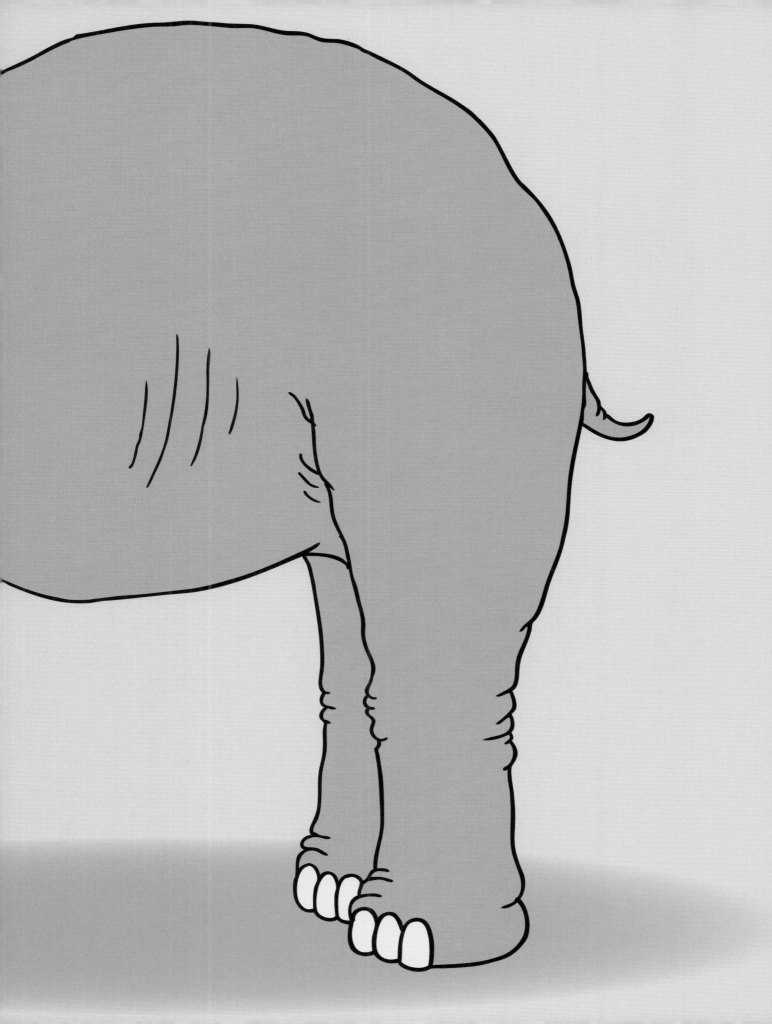

On the bus!

It was fun playing with my elephant in the backyard.

It was so fun taking my elephant for a walk in the park.

It was awesome fun taking my elephant to show-and-tell at school.

It was giggly fun tickling my elephant's tummy.

And it was messy fun building a house for my elephant.

But then my elephant got me into trouble.
It ate our neighbor's garden.

And my elephant was **not** house-trained.

And my elephant squashed our car.

Molly!

I decided that maybe a pet elephant was not such a good idea after all.

So I took my elephant back to the zoo.

When I got home, Polka was waiting for me.
Then I realized something. I already have the **perfect** pet;
the **perfect-size** pet. A pet that doesn't get me into trouble.
Which just goes to show, bigger is **not** always better.

**Although there are some things
that are better when they are bigger.
Like . . .**

Surprises!